Enjoy!

HAVE A DRINK,
HAVE A SMOKE

A TEACHER'S TALE

By the same author

A Stroke Of Luck Or A Beginner's Guide To Being
Hospitalised And What You Can Reasonably Expect!

Mrs Jay Meets The Creation Ratio:
A Pleasurable Cacophony Of Poetry

'Not Quite At That Level Yet': The Absurdity
Of Requirement. A Protest Of Experimental Poetry

HAVE A DRINK, HAVE A SMOKE

A TEACHER'S TALE

BY
CHRISTOPHER M. MOORE

ISBN: 978-1-917293-88-4

I was setting like the moon at midday, I was a contradictory apparition,

Like something was not right nor comprehended, less it offended.

Was I in bed for this awesome moment?

I guess so but did not know.

It appeared that I had all of the world leaders in my hand

Like Madame Le-Grande

And I had locked them all up in some grandiose gesture of revolution;

My absolution;

That was my solution.

I can re-call calling for the band:

The band, the band, I cried,

With the flower girls on shoulders, legs crossed like boulders

Around the willing necks of the sunglass folders

Happy for the close proximity of the seated;

Revelling in the beautiful moment they hoped to be repeated

But probably deleted

In the great scheme of things.

How sweet;

Thank you for the greet; thank you for the beauty of it all.

Not a register in sight

Not a parent in the night

Nothing but wristbands and music and cameras in the air

Only the band,

The band.

'Shit! What the fuck is that?'

My numbed arm slams the snooze button

And confetti drifts through my recovering mind.

'Shut the fuck up radio; give me a few more minutes please.

Have a heart, please, I beg you; Rick, I don't want to know right now

Not now;'

I must arouse myself but I will beg for three more minutes.

Interrupted again: 'for God's sake, let me be,

Let me lie here for a little while;

Just a little while; shut up Rick:

You are shut-up;

Thank you.'

Interrupted again; this time 'Sting'

Fuck it; another ex-teacher who escaped the ranks

And with gratitude said 'thank you but goodbye'

So now,

This time I am awake;

I adjust my position on the battlefield

Taking care not to disturb the enemy.

I hit the button again; let me fulfil the function of this button which says snooze.

The room stinks of last night's booze

But she, the enemy, continues to slumber, and in the meantime I have to wonder.

Can't afford to.

Can't spare the time to celebrate my ancestors; just let me lie here for a few more seconds

One last quiet moment

Before my stomach starts to wretch and churn

Meaning I search for the bucket strategically placed my side of the bed so not to disturb her.

The 'Thunderbirds' theme starts playing in my head;

Lady Penelope, Parker, and the Tracey brothers are go: gone to the circus

But

I am not

Yet I must be; I know it.

I clear my mind and have to get up. I am sweating right now; towing the safety line

And she is not awakened, or frightened by the remnants of last night, as I am.

A miracle, a time-lapse; I will call it anything right now;

For a few desperate seconds I am alone and love it.

It is now down to me to compose.

Yes; I am juggling kids and my lady who lies next to me, oblivious.

I must compartmentalise, strategically what it is I need to engage with my personality.

But, I do not have the ability; I don't have the nuance, as I lie here,

Seconds before I arise, tranquilised, traumatised, analysed;

Seconds before I despise.

Then, I think:

Do you know what?

I actually like the solitude of the moment

And when I said that line, took that line,

I believed it.

I watched it; full stage, got a sense of the wardrobe

Discovering sordid memories I did not want to wear anymore.

For a few more seconds before my day really starts

I'll let go a few farts; she won't notice; she's asleep.

And I think: she won't get the Norwich joke;

That's not the character I want to play.

No way.

I don't want to wear this, it reminds me of that sad occasion beyond my explanation.

I guess I am infringing on something,

Something I do not wish to infringe upon, and then its gone.

God; I feel sick, stomach cramps and regrets

Best I get me to a vet

Because I am an animal

Playing, toying, with accents;

Watching opera and playing hooky

Before I must get up.

Just a few more seconds please.

Very important that I do not disturb her snores; her dreams

So, slowly, carefully and with trepidation, I withdraw my side of the duvet

From my innocent body.

And it is cold; shit cold; bloody cold

Because it is too early for the heating to come on.

I ask myself: why am I so considerate?

Why am I making sure she still resides in a utopic state?

Don't know mate. Not sure.

Right.

On a logistical exercise;

Remove myself from the pit

And sit

On the edge,

Realising how cold it is.

Gather my senses, but still feel asleep.

I sit.

Bloody cold.

And my stomach begins to churn;

I feel that I must shit

Pretty damn quick.

But, I can't move at this very moment,

I am hit with anxiety:

Have I planned the lesson?

Have I prepared my confession?

Will I pick up the phone, and with disguised voice,

Say: I'm not well today; can't come in,

And here are my lesson plans for today.

If only I had a lesson plan.

Must leave my bed, my nest, my belligerent sleeping wife;

Must get to the loo; must have a crap.

Eventually I summon up the balls to exit the wedding bed;

Pull back the duvet on my side ,and hers is left untainted, unblemished.

I am up and witness the darkness,

I am up and remember what she said and I said and she said in response last night.

Never mind.

Creep, slowly and deliberately, remove myself from the space;

And go to another place, affectionally called the washroom, the wet room, the bog.

The sanctuary where I can think.

A cheap old radio resides on the shelf along with the toilet rolls;

Today, as I sit, I can't be bothered to stand; today, as I sit

Checking the burnt out cigarette butts and wondering whether I smoked them yesterday

And, looking for a light

I scratch a lonely match from the sodden box and re-ignite.

Cheap old radio plays out;

I doubt no-one is listening to the community radio, but it's got clout, apparently.

Puff, drag, puff drag; crap, but something is amiss; I wish I was pissed again but I am not.

I am shit scared of being a teacher, but that's my job; that's my lot.

I need a hanger to protect my manner;

Something is going wrong: something is not right; there is a fear to hit the light,

Probably chasing, probably just arrived, probably sat down, probably analysed,

Probably picked up nicely, and what do you surmise about he who does the work?

In complete precision, meticulous, scratching at the door,

A winner in the museum world, my temporary imprisonment is curtailed,

Like I had failed the deep dive.

But now what?

I have chosen to sit; I could have stood but I chose to sit.

I lever myself up; feel sick, but there's nothing I can do when I exit the loo

Except for dragging on the cigarette and making sure I do not disturb her.

And absent myself from the three buddhas and the rubber duck called Marc.

Poor old Marx; was once a trendy teacher, once, bit like me really.

A shower is now the order of the day;

This is the first time today that I am exposed and vulnerable.

As the water cascades, my body senses the poetical epiphany of it all

And the cerebral word play begins.

I am structured like a prisoner, deconstruction will not set me free;

The eloquent improvisation and the colour and the aggressive intimacy

Mean nothing to me.

I lather the gel into my hair and I become a fragile seer,

I know I am about to stumble into the wilderness; into the fear.

I let the water wash away the gel from my hair

And I stand there bare; I am at the centre of things

But my allotted four minutes is over.

Step out, embrace myself with a towel, and become dry.

Then I cry;

It happens every day of the working week and again on Sunday.

It is a frequent sadness; distinct, callous, malicious, obnoxious

And I soak it in silently,

No shouts, no whistles; I accept the ruling, I'm in for the ride:

I have always been swimming against the impossible tide,

But do not wish to be.

I look in the mirror; it is steamed, so, with a finger, I sketch a smiley face not smiling

Then wipe it away, which leaves a portal for me to witness my skewed portrait:

It's okay; shaved yesterday, day off today, but still apply the aroma of choice:

I let the towel drop to the floor; I am nude again.

However, not for long, as the towel is replaced with a bathing robe

And the towel is picked up, and draped over the cold radiator.

The shower is over for another day, but the tears are not;

The stomach churns again and I weave intimate soliloquies in my mind,

All about innovations, malpractices and minor victories,

Futures crafted by unkindness, bereft of any meaningful philosophy.

Lessons learnt; God knows I hate lessons and periods and free periods

Because a free period isn't free; it's your name pinned up on the board

By the deputy headteacher who has far more frees than you do

But his name is out of the equation, and yours is there instead.

That is the order of things and I am not even there yet;

No; I am navigating my way downstairs,

In the dark, in the cold, guided by the banister,

Towards a plastic fantastic show.

But I don't know what the storyline is today;

I can honour me legacy but don't know what to say.

I can traverse the stairs; I can go up or I can go down and I choose down

Down is the only way to go.

Down, drown; Down, down, down, drown; searching for the every man,

Down, drink a shot, down; drink another shot, down and drown.

Half way down; half way up; passed the eternal point,

Passed the immediate weavers and the disbelievers, passed the grey personae,

Shush; don't tell them I came,

Don't tell them I'm on the naughty step; don't tell them I am an intruder.

At the bottom of the stairs, I break into a sweat,

So light another cigarette

And dream of a drink.

Winners write the history, right?

Winners survive; keep the party alive,

I have no malfunctions, right?

I am just myself; burning on the last step, and I am truly down.

I can hear her slumbering; her blissful ignorance,

But I, the teacher, am up and operational in a wink

Longing for a drink,

Being myself, burning,

Before I sink again.

With meticulous scripting I wander wearily into the kitchen

Which offers an innocuous greeting seasoned from the night before.

Never mind; I don't take the show too seriously, there's always a sick comedy in it!

I contextualise the habitat, switch the light, reach for the kettle, turn on the tap,

Fill the kettle, turn off the tap, put the kettle on its base, flick the switch, and wait.

It's a process I undertake every day; it's approaching mediocracy,

But I am too afraid to be excited; surely it is time to amend the narrative,

Time to escape the mundane, time to dispel the emotional nuances of the hour.

Water boiled, poured diligently into the ageing teapot cast as Mrs Thatcher,

Tea bags added, one for each cup and one for the pot, as I was once told

Which means there are three in this marriage; my partner, the tea-pot, and I.

It takes precisely three minutes for the tea to mash so I put the time to good use:

Two stained mugs are selected from the cupboard;

Into each goes a dash of milk and one sugar; into the toaster go two slices of bread

And, with perfect synchronicity, both tea and toast present themselves as ready in harmony.

Next job, pour the tea into the two mugs, apply margarine and marmalade to the toast,

Take a bite of said toast, take another and another, then a sip of tea, then another, another.

Turn on the TV which spits out its venom of testing material,

Talking of how the streets are full of sushi

And that we're all acting like toddlers on too much sugar; what a vilified conception!

And that there's a weather warning today for high wind.

God; I am pissed off,

Dear God, I am considering un-plugging myself,

And I must give up these

But not today.

A pristine box of cigarettes is broken into, one is selected, and placed between my lips;

I lean over the hob, turn the gas on, light a ring, approach said ring with precision,

Position cigarette over the blue flame, draw in, turn off the gas, and 'AAHHH.'

In the moment, I almost forgot, but, no: next job;

Few more drags, few more sips, few more bites, then deliver my wife's beverage, in bed.

'About ten past seven dear, good morning.'

No reply

'Here's your tea dear.'

No reply

'Chris to wife, Chris to wife, do you read me, over!'

And do you know what?

I am overwhelmed with jealousy and a bitter rage;

Why is it not me unaware of the world?

Why is it me who hits the plateau, who fears the creative mediation?

Why is it me who uses time; with it, without it, and other orchestrations?

Why is it not me in the optimum condition,

Picking the low hanging fruit, enjoying easy options?

Why is it me with diminishing hope?

Why is it me learning to be vertical again, and not you:

'I'll just leave it here then'

'Thanks'

A reply; a veritable ripple of reaction.

'What time is it?'

'About ten past seven.'

There is a sense of a gentle life force trickling through her veins,

A sweet innocence,

At one,

Whereas I am afraid to get on the bus because there are too many people on it

'Do you want me to call you again in a few minutes?'

'No'

The monosyllabic response rips through my soul,

'I'll get up when I've drunk this.'

Do what you want to do, I think, but dare not say,

Failing to cope with her gymnasium of expression emerging from her muscular mind.

Open the wardrobe, withdraw the pre-determined garments, and leave the rest behind.

Yesterday happened, tomorrow will happen, but can today go away?

Must I be part of the victim culture; must I strip myself to the bare bones again?

I've lost my rap to a tripper; never wanted this endless weapon endeavour;

I never refuted the detail; never denied the voices in my head, never spoke, never said.

So not to disturb her without good reason, I enter the spare room

And start the process of donning my armour; soon I am resplendent in suit.

I go back to the kitchen, back to the loaf; fix myself some pathetic sandwiches

Then wrap them in clingfilm and put them in my school bag along with the exercise books

Belonging to 8X and 10Y.

Now it is time for the next task, the necessary task, the numbing task:

The ritual of the hip flask.

I know this would be frowned upon if anybody knew; perhaps they do, I don't know.

She is still upstairs, I have checked,

So I seek out the golden 40% by volume,

Carefully pour the safety liquid into the flask

And place the flask in my jacket inside pocket, and re-hide the old stag.

The ritual is over for another day,

This time, I don't cry, I sigh; a sigh of relief and comfort.

I am inert.

I have a few seconds to waste

So I sit, and ponder; strange, weird thoughts engulf me, tsunami-like:

When the dream becomes reality; I've been there a dozen times,

All of the rays of the sun were black; a commitment to anarchy was made,

A journey down the drain, up the chimney down, and down the chimney up,

I know the scene, it's handleable; it's hung in the trees and posted on the rails,

It never fails; the fate is in the mystery.

'Morning'

I am sprung from my state of comatose.

'Morning; sleep alright?'

Of course she did; she always does; demons ignore her and concentrate on me.

She is in the room with me now; in my domain, in my personal space,

But I like it. I like her smell.

She is pretty; as pretty as the picture of a pretty lady that hangs in the lounge,

Our pretty lounge, our pretty place.

She is also an enigma; like an unrecognised telephone number,

She is the end of a fifty year question mark.

Collectively, we are trapped in the moment.

She moves nearer,

Like she's moving in for the kill.

'Want another cup of tea?; should be one in there.'

She nods. I find another mug, add the pre-requisites, pour and offer it to her,

Symbolic of a religious gift.

At this time of day, it is impossible to talk with meaning or intent.

'Good day?'

She speaks, but now it is my turn not to answer:

Good day? Good bloody day? You are kidding, aren't you?

If one is in the gutter, one can only look at the stars because what's the point of lying there

Asking for someone to kick you?

Good bloody day?

'As always', I lie.

Unhappy with this unanticipated turn of events; I make my escape:

'Got to get ready.'

She steps away from me, but her smell remains,

I shuffle back the chair and stand, ready to leave.

And I leave the stage; what is it about performers who look for applause

When they know none will be forthcoming?

That scene was just rank bad,

Awkward in the extreme.

She sits on the chair I had occupied as if she has usurped me

And sips on her tea, nonchalantly, alone with her thoughts and ideas.

Before the next scene commences, I sit on the bottom step of the stairs and think:

I met her in 1975 at Uni;

At the students union meeting for freshers, they said one in four of us would meet

Our partners here, and how we laughed.

It was not love at first sight; far from it,

She pursued me, I did not pursue her.

But then, a thing called love took over

And she continued to pursue me

And I pursued her.

I was captivated by her sweetness and her smell.

Brief look at my wrist-watch;

No, I'm still okay

And she's eating toast now

I'm okay, and don't move from the step.

How I wish I could stay on the step, the naughty step,

And go nowhere, but stay within the depths of my mind.

I don't want to go to school,

The anticipation of it makes me sick and nervous.

I want to remain on the step and stare into the ether

I want school to go away

I'd rather go hunting Puffins

And watch old programmes of Muffin the Mule

On TV.

I wish Zebedee would suddenly appear

And, with a spring in his step, declare 'it's time for bed.'

Another brief look at my wrist-watch;

Time to move; time to say good-bye to her.

Even though there is something she is not telling me;

Something for me to be mindful of, something to find;

And I'm like a cook in a care home, like a drunk in a gin bar,

I am confused, searching for the bigger, holistic strategy,

Begging for a category to align the jar.

It has become a destination again; a ping chef, with a glass of wine,

Deluding myself with feeling fine.

I am a crime waiting to happen, taking myself back to the moment;

Swinging in and swinging out,

Watching tutorials on line,

Wearing a pinny, murmuring a prayer, searching for the buoyancy aid,

Blown out from sex but fishing for the mortal bite,

And the zero possible fight is misconstrued; she won't inform me,

So I pursue the boyhood dream, wondering why the beauty queen is whittled down

To a landing site

And why I feel she fights me for no reason at all.

In my mind, in my torment,

I am in a Limo in L.A.

I am taking a holiday from school;

I am familiarising myself with a broader, more complex, agreement

Whereby the experience is one of reluctant freedom.

I am overseeing the day but don't want it that way;

I sense a nervous energy about the place.

'Bye then'

'Bye'

'Back after the meeting'

'Okay'

'About six I suppose'

'Okay.'

Exit left and centre with a mutually turned cheek to receive a gratuitous excuse of a kiss,

Exit left and centre with car keys retrieved from the top of the G-Plan telephone seat,

Exit left and centre from the cold inside to the cold outside,

Exit left and centre; shut the door behind.

Escape.

Walk the few steps to the car, push the fob, door unlocks.

I enter this new but familiar world.

Shuffle, belt on, key into ignition, switch, lift -off.

I'm straight off a plane, straight into the game; Thunderbirds are a go-go.

I don't want to be pitied, don't want to be defined,

Don't want to let others pre-determine my mind,

Don't want to know what is amiss.

Don't 'get' the sad references;

Don't want to do it; want to hide, want to be absent, confined,

Guess I knew but never tried

To get to the truth of it: bloody shit!

And then, 'what?'

What if, what should, what could?

And, for God's sake, I have moved nowhere yet.

The engine turns but I'm still immobile.

Never mind.

Gear engaged; movement towards another day on the chalkface.

It's an extraordinary goodbye but I don't know why.

I feel disconnected. I am confetti at a wedding.

I am on a guilt trip; I am going to work, delusional, confused.

Never knew why I veered around like a shopping trolley;

Never really guessed why the sun and happiness excluded me.

I never knew the glory hole was a lane;

Never trod the footpath; never looked around.

But I want to live to one hundred and five;

I want to be alive to categorise my emotions and commotions;

I want to keep on breathing and believing

That there is one more day, two, three, four days, to the weekend, my friend.

Still inert, sat in my car and my mind is going afar,

Brilliantly, brilliantly, brilliantly afar,

Considering brilliant ideas and stupid ideas

While the fears are still there, squared, uncomposed, up the nose

And buzzing like a silent disco; buzzing, buzzing, constant humming,

Drumming, drumming; constant humming,

Reminiscent of the Irish dance, strumming: so random, so becoming

Of the little family where tragedy abounds and the hounds get lost and go missing.

Before I move, I am looking for the perfect sanctuary;

I am searching for the perfect theatre, placing myself in the royal box.

But, of course, it cannot be; you see, I am in the driver's seat of my car.

Check mobile: nothing. Turn the radio on. Nothing really, just bland background

But it's good enough.

Can't even 'man spread' in here, in my tin cage; can't classify my rage,

Can't share with the group but I can drive;

I have to drive, I need to drive, but don't want to be alive;

No chance today to skive;

Today is my mission to survive one more day.

Today I will be that teacher.

Today I will make you proud of me.

I reverse the car out of the drive; out of my mind and pull out onto the road,

The route I know and I peer through the misty window,

Ready to drive to another demise.

I start another trip; transfixed on the route ahead, blinded by the headlights

And the rain and the refrain on the radio intoxicates me.

I drive to another surmise and wonder; I wonder, I wonder,

The rumour mill is in overdrive; pink jazz Louis fills a space with blues,

And what's the news?; don't know, don't care.

It was this week two years ago; was hard to keep it quiet,

I faced a challenge; involved in riot.

Told my Mum and Dad; they were stunned; he on a diet and compliant with my choice

To express my voice referencing the best day ever; the new class of twenty-three,

You, and me; the roller-coaster, the military precision, wanting to be intimate

But learning what it is to plea; needing to pull it off and get together,

Whatever the weather as the rain hits my windscreen and the wipers cool what I find.

I know the quotes; not so many rehearsals though; two years ago, pushing forty,

Something nice and something naughty; exaggerate expressions but had it all;

Why didn't you ask me twenty years before?

Why didn't you ask me to demonstrate?

Was it all too complicated for you?

Shite!

Red light.

Back in the world for a moment.

I know the trip, I know the route.

Orange, Green: time to go back into the sequence again.

Nothing to prevent me from lighting up, nothing stopping my train of thoughts,

Nothing checking the ills and the noughts, nothing judging what I taught

Or learnt about myself over these God-forsaken years of sincerity tears.

Oh; the cool smoke, the joyous aroma, the knowledge, the insight,

The creation and realisation of what is right,

Behind the wheel of this car as I travel to somewhere I do not want to be;

I want to be free of this trip.

Out of the world I go again; I can predict this route;

I will traverse it innocently and I will concentrate; proud to wear my suit.

I am now gentle and mellow; wrecked by memory and anticipation,

Yet petrified; should have been a solicitor or a local government official

Or something trivial like a bank clerk, or any other pen-pusher,

But instead of that, I chose to be a teacher,

I chose a pot of honey, a hug and a Vodka;

I chose nirvana; I chose gravitas and respect and idealism:

Iconic idealism and utopia.

Did some research the other day;

I lived in one road and you lived near to me.

I dreamt about you

And predicted a downfall

Which materialised in an unfortunate screw of fate.

Must concentrate

Must engage;

Must.

The road is not a dream

But the consequence is.

Don't want any thoughts to rape my mind

That would be unkind.

At any time of day that would be liable for a fine.

This town and that town, that village, that open space,

Going past the bloke with the twisted face.

This road, that road; that house, that disgrace:

I know the places I voyage through.

I am accustomed to this particular trip

And my mind meanders again.

I stand in front of a class but I feel like a ghost,

I try to teach them something but I feel like I know nothing.

I smile and crack a joke but feel like crying,

I praise and encourage but guess I am dying.

I used to respect my charges but now they just don't care,

I want to make a difference but feel that I'm not there.

And then I go home every day but sense I have no place,

I try to find some solace, but find I have no grace.

I suffer from depression, but know I just can't tell,

I want to ask for help, but sure, I'm deep in hell.

I am a depressed teacher; I am the depressed preacher,

I'll try to meet you but it must be on my terms

So that you and I can both learn

About the futility of it all.

I am a depressed teacher;

I'd love to meet you

But it would have to be on my terms.

I am alone,

I am unknown,

I have consequence,

I seek recompense

As my trip continues.

Did I clock that the other day?

Is it safe to say I missed it yesterday?

Never mind.

I dreamed of being a teacher but I did not know the reality.

I wanted to inspire and educate, but couldn't fathom the difficulty.

I faced a system that was broken but didn't know how to fix it,

I spoke to pupils troubled but didn't suss how to reach them.

I have worked long and hard hours but didn't trust who I'd blame

Because for them and me and all between, it felt like a game

Without balance, but full of malice,

Don't talk of her; don't mention Alice,

Don't evoke the poisoned chalice

Who lives in the palace just up the road from the school.

She is so young, but suffers no fools; she has all the tools in her box

To bring down the whole damned lot,

And she would, because she could.

I don't know how to cope; should I hang from a rope like a coward?

I have lost my passion, my motivation

And I don't know how to regain them.

I am frustrated.

I am hopeless.

I am disillusioned.

I am depressed.

I am a depressed and disillusioned teacher,

I am the depressed and disillusioned teacher

Only half way through my drive

But still I guess alive

So that is something I suppose; who knows?

Always the white queen, with disassociated memories,

Always the matriarch of the street and there's always the marker on the map.

On this magical voyage, the landscape changes but the vocalisations are constant,

Pushing as far as they possibly dare, rolling back on the big commitment,

Explaining that the route to the stars and the route to Spar is one of the same thing,

Whereby you pull out the plant and pull out the weed at the same time,

And, driving my car an auto, I'm sat on the grass in a silent woodland,

Creating spaces and confusing criteria, re-imagined and quite spectacular,

Designing my own badge and popping the blister pack.

Out of the windscreen, I see the vibrant light,

A cacophony of colours, dancing, shrill and bright,

As the shapes and images shift so fast,

Progressing to the cosmic vast.

I feel the music coursing through my veins,

I sense the symphony of joy and pain

And my emotions are thrust to the surface

Riding the roller-coaster of self-purpose.

I taste the bitterness of the air,

A flavour of the earth: I'm there.

Digging down and tempting vice,

Scent of memory, sense of spice.

Dreams and visions and hopes and fears,

Collages of the few and dear

Which reach for the essence of my wearisome soul,

Convulsions vibrate, touch the hole.

I will photo-bomb every photograph I can photo-bomb,

I promise to start every conversation with a taboo or an innuendo, if you prefer.

I will grow into my face; I will be a feather-faced disgrace; I will sing a song.

Zombified; that is what I have become,

Dead to everything and everyone around me but in some way alive.

And now it is the ritual of the motorway drive,

The anonymous, repetitive ribbon of grey and dappled concrete awaits my distraction,

As I pick up speed to match those around me.

And the miles fly by; this is my escape,

Perhaps now I can find my space; forlornly I hope, but no;

The dreaded tedium sets in, the inevitable tedium grows,

I feel that I am driving with nowhere to go,

I feel that I am committing a fearful mistake.

Now is not the time for unrealistic claims and debauchery,

Now is not the time for hunting Puffins,

Now is not the time to ask 'just what are the people saying?'

Now is not the time to throw it all in the air and see what comes down

Now is not the time to question 'is it all me?'

The motorway is not my escape; it is my enemy,

And the humble humming of the engine forces me to struggle with self-doubt,

Now is not the time to ponder 'what's it all about?'

Light up, inhale, hold, exhale,

Fill the tin can with putrid but perfect white smoke

And I like the smell and become mindful

So what the hell? ; life is tranquil,

Inhale; slowly, peacefully, majestically,

Hold; hold everything still in total peace and blissfulness,

And exhale; with purpose, creating rings,

And repeat, repeat, repeat until nothing is left.

Nothing remains, just a machine and I, suffering the motorway.

Exceptional receptor; the perfect maelstrom comes into view.

It waits for me, mysteriously beguiling me; calling me, tempting me as it stands alone, cold.

The bridge is a picture of something different, as if granting me an unrequested privilege

Which is not as routine as it might look on first glance.

So, I approach with trepidation and, as Simon and his mate once said 'I will lay me down',

I will ponder Bobbie's muddy waters, murders and dead babies,

I will re-iterate the question posed by James: 'Can I take it to the bridge?'

This bridge I encounter every day; it is a bond between two disparate realms,

One which pushes, one which pulls.

This bridge is part of my quest; a trial that begs to be met with zest yet disappears in flames.

It is both an impediment and an aim, a cause of strife or some acclaim.

It is an allegory of my fate; it is a stretch of bliss or hate, depending on my direction.

The bridge is a constant and I am half-way there, in no-man's land,

Neither here, neither there; betwixt the two, over the water,

Masking the certain space:

Formidable. Awesome. A masterpiece of technology

With a soul all of its own which tantalises and plays with my raw emotions,

Creates a fearful commotion with my dreads and fears.

And, just like any other day, as I prepare to exit the bridge, push to exit its grasp,

The lump in my throat returns

And the tears flow again.

I know that the bridge is my partner until our final date;

It will never be a haven of solace or peace,

Neither will it be a spot to pause or release.

It is a remnant; it is a vision,

It is a part of who I am; it is my decision.

I will lay me down, I will submit.

Late, I am late leaving the bridge. I care, but should not care;

Yes, I must be in time; teacher contracts and all that,

But I have travelled miles; I am not local,

I can't be a PE teacher and surf the waves at three,

No, for me, is this complexity of a trip and an urge to be free.

Time?

I'm Okay.

Shouldn't be in trouble?

No.

And I want my wife back,

I fear she does not want me.

I need my wife right now

But I guess she does not need me,

Something I sensed; something was wrong,

I guessed the words, I wrote the song.

This is my kitchen; this I my limp wrist,

Before you accuse me of it.

Time? Yes, on time, always have been,

Always fucking have been.

Drive, baby, drive to your profession, drive to your confession;

Guess the imposition which awaits you.

But those are not my words and I miss my wife

Safely wrapped up in time,

And I'm not feeling fine; not good at all.

I am on the rock now; I am an island. An island on an island. The paradox hurts.

I might as well be a million miles from home right now, for what it's worth,

Because, this morning, something was different;

Something was strained, the air was full of foreboding,

Something got to me in an incomprehensible manner.

I sense a spectre looming above my head.

It is a black and menacing figure that fills my soul with dread,

And persuades me to doubt my vigour.

The sky has turned dark, the sea has turned red, the stars have fallen down, the moon is black.

The planets fade and doubt;

I wonder what this craziness is about.

I just can't figure it out: what it is or from whence it came, this thing undefined

But can only surmise it is malign;

It whispers in my ear of impending doom

And makes me feel misaligned, like some sort of treacherous sign.

I strive to cast it off, exorcise the demon, try to be valiant

Yet it adheres to me, feeds off me, like a sucking parasite,

It saps my hope and strength away. I am out of sight.

It is a portent, it is a hex; it is a portent and a trial, it is vile;

I am truly vexed, deprived of even a meaningless smile.

I have journeyed mile after mile now, day after day, week after week,

Month after month, year after bloody year

And when I become an island, when I lay me down, when the paradox begins,

The nausea intensifies; I wretch with boring regularity.

I can see her face, she stares through me; cold as ice,

Then she turns away as if that's suffice, but I still don't get it and the trip is forlorn.

Forget that for now.

I traverse the final few miles,

And very soon, the lofty tower looms,

Piercing the dank and dreary skyline

Like a monument celebrating the air of gloom.

I know the tales it can narrate; I know the sorcery it can create,

These things I know, and I yield to its seduction. I am the bait.

But who am I kidding?

This is no lofty tower; this is no place of solace,

This is a school;

This is the culmination of another petrifying trip,

This is the situation of confrontation,

Much less an edifice of education.

This is a space for speculation, condemnation, accusation, differentiation,

Dissatisfaction, incomprehension, disorientation, contamination,

Mortification, exasperation, degradation, rejection,

Coercion, disruption, destruction,

Abduction, addiction, aggression,

Alienisation, apprehension, asphyxiation,

Aversion, demonisation,

Dehumanisation;

This is an awful place to be.

I pull up in the empty car park; I gather my books, my bags, my thoughts.

I lock the car door. I check it's locked. I pace towards the uninviting entrance.

I inhale deeply; the cold air bites my throat and chars my lungs.

I enter the code, I push on the door and I am ushered in;

By what, I do not know; it's not as if I want to be here. I pass through. I am in.

Early, too early; I don't want to go that far.

The smell of the place: Head's smoke, Deputy's smoke, my smoke

And a hundred others' smoke lingers in the air. The pupils' confiscated smoke

Attacks my senses like a dark tornado. I hit a hurdle.

I am running for a genuine medal; I don't want to pass real slow;

I'll take a shove, the gaps are going backwards;

In any case, it just won't be confirmed. That much I have learned.

Got to watch the last one; got to charge my fate.

Got to ask how far is it; got to get the space.

Got to be the favourite, but I 'aint'

Got to watch the time.

My God; it stinks in here.

Echoed bellies watching tellies,

56, enjoyed 68 to 73, turned on 74, tuned in 75 to 78

Doctor this and Doctor that; Doctor coughing, Doctor dread. Doctor: Dead.

It was too tough to watch; we ate peculiar jellies.

I cross the threshold; I am not carried, this is not a marriage
But it may as well be one, created in hell.

'I take you, teaching, to be my beloved wife.'
'Do you take me? Yes? How? In what form?
'I am married, after all.'

'Are you; are you really? Don't you feel contrary?'

The stench of this place really gets me in a bad way.

Help me; this glorious place, this den of iniquity, envelops me

As I pace myself towards in theory my sanctuary.

And you know what they say: schools are lovely places when they are empty;

So beautiful, so fatalistic, so pessimistic, so unforgiving,

So driven; looking for the biggest mark,

With the maze charting where it was.

Help me; this poor copy attacks me,

You are in no way beautiful, but beguiling.

Yes, I drove my car here, I was driving at the time,

I was doing Cluedo up north.

I didn't crash the car; just had a call

And, wow, yes; it was possible

Like being in the shower, like making the right decision.

Like being planned properly; with precision,

Like making the final incision,

I drove my car here.

This is my classroom. This is the scene of my battles;

I enter and survey the scream; somewhere I have often been

And, My God; I hate it.

I think: in a few hours' time, this room will be invaded by reluctant volunteers

Who, like me, would rather not be here

But, at the moment, I am in no-man's land and I sort of like it.

Wall displays? No

Time to play? No

Chance for a distraction? Yes

I light up

I light up,

And fade away for the briefest of moments; far away, so far away

Then open the windows and let the fun dissipate,

Re-position behind my desk, my barrier,

Sitting triumphantly, reluctantly; wondering where's my mate.

It just kind of happened of course,

When I was actually alive;

I kind of went like that on my own merit.

I had gone away,

I was cryptically camouflaged

But searching for the unconnected and the confetti,

Begging for the motivational speaker and the spaghetti,

Re-adjusting behind my desk, my barrier,

My defence, my white line from whence it will be just fine

In the circumstantial time

Of vulnerability.

Okay; enough of that, you stupid prat!

I push back my chair; it squeals like it only does in a school.

I stand erect. Fine with no-one there.

I am not scared, but will be soon,

Come the afternoon.

I walk around the room; read the scribblings on the desk:

'T Loves J' and 'S The best'

And, 'for sex call B'

And 'for pills, check Phil's'

This is what it has come to, this noble profession.

I need someone to hear my confession,

I've been scammed.

So confused; I hear the voice ghosts and fear the worst;

I am damned. I am consequence. I guess the rest;   the important items are misplaced

Within both sides of the equation,

Like the question of Ibiza, the chance of Caesar, the insignificance of it all.

I will walk to the staff room.

I will hit the teachers' retreat,

The staff room. I will open the door. I will enter

And no-one is there. It is now my domain.

If you think you're too old, think again;

I sold out before the festival began,

I went back on bad material; I surmised it's not available,

I cried and wriggled in the cradle

And was stopped going out at night to check the refrain.

Walking to the solace, walking to my face, walking to the pit, walking to disgrace,

Walking to the staff room, walking to my space,

My chair, my seat; we say hello and greet

From our allotted graces, yet not one is here right now.

I am walking the walk from one shit place to another, to the teachers' retreat.

Can't read the words, can't read the philosophy or the mind-set,

Can't digest the union crap on the walls; I've heard it all.

Get a coffee, quick; no-one here to manipulate my mind,

Quick smoke; no-one cares,

I am re-butted; my mind is shut out

But do I care? Not at this exact moment, no. A picture of my troubles grows.

Bleak ? it really is inside here; I should do a deep dive into the documents

Pinned on the wall but I won't just now; it is too early,

There is no-one else here, I will repose in my allotted place and think

About a tranquil way of life with a troubled warm-up,

With a proud history ; mending and healing the un-opened wound

But being angry about it won't change much in this God-forsaken staff room.

I could walk around here like a ghost; I could hide under a bridge,

I could get stale milk from the fridge

And I could speak to someone who really understands, but no-one is here.

Before, during and after the service, all is lost in the compelling backdrop,

Bleak? Bleak indeed.

I think:

I am a surviving person; out of my comfort zone, out of my depth but surviving,

I am up against the environment closing in on me;

I am getting it in the ear; and I cried around the kitchen table when I was able,

Cried for hours and hours and hours; special, buzzing, amazing: allowed,

Because of the unforgiving crowd.

So there is no point in covering the English act;

There is too much sound in the truck and it is hot like bread;

Wish I was in my bed; wish I could engage with my head, but I can't.

It won't be long until I am on the stage.

I will be Christopher!

I will be 'Sir' without a citation

I will be me in disguise,

I will surmise and analyse

I will peruse through un-seeing eyes,

I will go on tour.

Each day is the same, so I will watch the clock and wait, until the silence is surrendered.

The door opens:

'Morning Chris'

'Morning Ellie'

'You okay?'

'I'm cool: you?'

'Saw a programme on the TV last night: they like their baubles in Brid!'

'Didn't catch that'

'They were talking about being hot under a stylish collar.'

'Really?'

'They said you could get Vitamin D via the TV'

'Wow!'

'Want a coffee?'

'Yes please!'

Ellie moves to the space where coffee is made and consumed;

Disappear Ellie, forever on view: always the first, never the last, but she is not teacher

But a teacher's best friend. A trusted compatriot on the battle front,

Who accepts me as I am; with question, but without judgement.

Soon she will bring me the coffee in a stained and chipped mug but I don't care,

Yet again, I am going somewhere.

Only kids communicate across the divide; playing the alien, surfing the drive,

Pulling sullen faces, messing around; channelling the concept of all that's alive,

Connecting with troubles; festering with the high times and lazy chimes and

Back to Earth; considering the curve-ball.

'Have you heard what I said at all?'

'Sorry Ellie; my mind's not quite in gear, my dear'

'Drink your coffee before it gets cold'

'Thank you. Thank you so much, and what's the time?'

Eradicate the response; it is meaningless now because I know the time to the minute.

The door swings open again, and enters belligerent Tim.

His son attends Eton, you know, or so he claims.

He has an Antique Shop in Lewes; such is his refrain.

He has bawled me out on inspection,

Then claimed it was all a game

To suss me out, to spook me, to suggest I should re-train.

He was the bastard in my frame, but we passed; he said he was insane

To question my ability and we should let sleeping dogs lie; I was fine by that.

'Morning Elle, morning Chris'

'Morning Tim' in unity.

I hate this guy, my unfortunate colleague,

I am forced to work with him, and by him, and through him: mine is the intrigue

But at least he is regular and I think again.

When you are in space, what should you play?

When you are sitting in a cubicle far, far away;

If it is another day, how could you possibly pray

Without being manipulated by the sentence,

Listening to the hearsay and the tray of words laid out beside the fence?

It's been a surreal struggle to get this far;

I've drunk some wine and put my slippers by the fire

But then I ask where am I going; Tenerife or other showings?

Where am I at right now; why am I dimming the stars by a fraction?

What is my given reaction?

There are three Tim's in the room.

Me, Ellie and the moon.

Now is the occasion for the world to go round and around,

Round and around; open, shut; round and around and around;

Open, shut, open, shut; round and around goes the rotating door

With the lambs being spat out of it like an eating dis-order;

Lambs to the slaughter; some smile, some grimace,

Some don't want to show their face;

All burdened with emotional backlash. It is the veritable parade.

It is the entrance of my colleagues, the teachers, who look as bad as me.

For my part, I am obsessed by the music in my head, but I say 'hello'

But I'm playing a theme; weaving a breath together.

And the words and the texts are so poignant in my mind,

Destined to be tantalising incomplete.

What happens when it stops?

I don't have a clue; do you?

I have been abandoned by distraction; I've sought the torso and chunks of reaction,

I have incorporated mutuality; I have witnessed the imaginary museum; fought manipulation:

I suppose the silence is finished; I long for the final episode.

This place is now a hubbub of activity,

Discussions of lost days, and who to praise.

We say 'hello' to each other yet blank out the response,

We are all on auto-pilot.

I don't like it.

'Ellie, I'm not liking this; not one little bit.'

'It's a new day'

'I still don't like it; need a shit'

'Another one?'

'**A**nother one; well, not strictly; just a wee. Too much coffee!'

And off I go on a familiar journey; to the loo – to the 'Gentleman's' repose,

The toilet which reeks of violet blocks – the space which gets up my nose

But offers a place to hide away; to suppose, to compose the thoughts of a fall.

These are converted children's facilities: the urinals are too low, the seats too small,

The cubicle doors? Forget them! Ankles and pants can be spotted underneath,

And above the door, your face and teeth are visible to all who want a look!

Forget professionalism! Forget the noble calling; this is appalling

But it is the state of things.

Enter filthy dirty wretched space. Lock door. Trousers and pants down.

I cannot bring myself to pee into the urinal. Then I start to think.

This is personal to me, like a swimming challenge or something colder,

Like climbing the stairs or climbing a mountain or something bolder;

This is the slow-motion version; I've seen the other immersions,

I wear my heart on my jumper; I've got the knitting pattern,

I can give you the juicy gossip; the issues of distraction:

I am the curator, the guide: under the piano I hide,

Getting friendly with the environment and I confide.

I accidentally fell in love: yes, definitely, I fell in love by chance.

I had no sense; it was a passive romance.

It was like walking into the living room but nothing was there,

I was in a trance

But I forget the first dance

And I left it to chance.

Finished. Pants up. Trousers up. Door unlocked,

Leave the facility which reeks of violet blocks.

Kick the door of the staffroom open; find my designated place,

The worn out chair that is allotted to me and my face;

Sit right down with a sigh, pick up yesterday's paper and read:

'Stonedhenge' : so ironic. I blow and I climb; I think of Aunt Mary,

I think of the tea and the weeds in my garden;

I sit on the grass and beg for your pardon.

The prison I am in is not working; how could a whale be a Russian spy?

How can I conquer the first night nerves; why should I try?

School has always been a priority, along with 'Il Forno's'

But it's a dark place to be; will be the end of me.

I have a feeling: this is not going to be a typical day; no way.

The change I've seen in students over time is difficult to define.

And I have become completely reclusive; unable to shine,

I have been catapulted into the limelight: not a good gig for a disillusioned guy.

In my imagination, I was at the first preview last night; I cried through most of it.

I played with music; pulsing, throbbing, digging the scene

If you know what I mean, and I laughed; I laughed a belly laugh

Straight from the bowels of the philharmonic staff.

'Chris, Chris: it's pinned on the board.'

'Okay; thanks for the warning Ellie.'

We are supposed to be a noble profession, but I've got a little confession to make.

This is the time of day every teacher fakes.

We pretend to be all nonchalant but inside we wish we could have our say.

Does it have to be this way? I anticipate the fall;

I prepare to pay homage to the wall: to see the inevitability of it all.

I am not filled with anything akin to optimism bias as I walk the plank;

And the battle-orders are there in their glory, placed with precision

By the man with the mission; the man of attrition; oblivious to the derision,

Leaving us all anonymous; nowhere to be seen – not part of this desperate scene.

The General has plotted this in his mews; his scheme to torture and abuse.

The soldiers dread in the camp, to face the horror and the damp.

I sharpen my blades and my spikes; brave the slaughter and the strike;

Might as well be on my bike.

The General, the Deputy Head is the stuff of nightmares, the sarcastic words he has said.

He plays with my soul; he infiltrates my head. He is the tyrant of the school,

But he's no fool as he breaks every rule;

He is the chief tormentor; his is the main-man bully;

He is the dictator, he is the schemer.

It is he who sets the 'goals', the strategies', the 'mission' of this place,

He is the ultimate disgrace, represented by these daily battles orders,

The cover rota; instructing who's due to lose face and in who's room.

This is my fate and I'll learn it soon.

The General revels in taking our time and making our hackles rise

Whilst he hides in his office; rarely to be seen again, feeling ever so wise.

'Gone again'

'Oh shit; not them again!'

'She's always off this day!'

'Why can't the General take his turn?'

'You're having a bubble, aren't you?'

'Bugger it!'

It is in this way that the General has set the professional tone of the day;

His battle-orders sealing our fate; thoughts of massacre and retreat set to hold sway.

Cruel fate; c'mon mate, let me off this once!

Not a chance, not a flying fig; my free succumbs,

And so do I; retreat to my allotted space, give good grace
and fly.

But, I am staying in my head; I try resting in my head;

I'm in a terrible place; still working myself out,

Curious to know what I'm worried about:

'Do you want to share what's wrong with me?'

There's only so much a teacher can do in class.

Am I living comfortably? Am I Floyd-like numb?

Do I take in what you say? Must I succumb?

Nobody will talk about it; no-one's having fun.

The trip has taken me years to understand;

To know my place, guess where just I stand.

Now, I walk out of the room; feeling lighter

But worried by the child;

I'm on the waiting list – call me Lisa –

I will do my best to please you.

Right now, I'm selective mute,

Sort of insane, sort of cute,

Working through the situation,

Coming off the stage: it's all the rage, you know!

I can't meet the demand; I will stay in my head,

I'm in a terrible place.

I will be simultaneously referred;

I am brittle.

I cannot

Think

Any more, and am not let off.

Kicked twice; once is not enough:

I am reminded by many whose turn is not there's but mine;

It is time for my appointed, my anointed, playground duty.

Not likely to react with a joyous emotion; more likely a fuddled confusion.

And the howling wind strikes across the concrete jungle wasteland

Which I enter with trepidation from the sanctuary of the condemned

Whereby I am chilled to the bone, and start to listen to the screams in the distance,

And the yelps of pain with mocking taunts; the lost soul approaching

Dragging haunts; tugging on my soul. my sleeve, my make believe, encroaching

Disposing; clinging to my hand which I pull away in disgust and contempt.

I do not wish to know: I am not comfortable with crowds and the freezing temps;

The random acts of violence aborted from my mind.

I

Stand

Alone.

What should I do out here?

The decision is made:

I am out here because of consequence; no one cares.

They are happy to avoid the bullet, my professional friends.

So, I huddle deeper, deeper, deep into my fleece lined anorak,

Waiting for the appropriate time to blow the whistle;

The perfect hour to bring this sham to an end:

What can I do out here?

Right now; no one's looking. The kids are oblivious to the teacher's curse;

The staff-room windows hold pepper faced creatures in verse,

So my chance is here to fly; don't know why but I have to try; to trip,

To escape. I light up. I am a naughty boy and sup from the alloy: you there Nurse?

I accept the fairies and the contraries; I feel no need to be involved with the conflicts

And the petty rivalries. I resist that which should be a temptation to jump in and mediate.

D'you know what? I can't be arsed to contemplate my refusal to procrastinate

About my failure to ask: 'How do you feel about that?', and 'How could you compromise?'

And 'what do you think you should do next?'

I don't bloody care! Scream it loud and clear! I am done with my pastoral responsibility!.

I don't want to enforce boundaries; I don't care if things get out of control,

I am a Teacher, not an enforcer. I am not a Police Officer;

Nor a social worker, nor a crowd control operative, nor a Medic, nor nothing else;

I am supposed to be a teacher; not even a mobile phone confiscator.

I will not lie as I stand windswept and alone. The draws pass through and I breathe,

Oblivious to the cut knees and the sullen pleas tugging, tugging on my sleeve incessantly,

Never, ever leaving me alone: never leaving me alone.

I see it all now, perfectly:

Opening bananas, smoking areas; broken locks and smashed up doors,

Disgusting ravages; polished floors:

Time to reveal the scenario cards: the friendship, falling out, conflict cards,

The resolving cards: because in this yard, this den of iniquity, everything stinks.

Far away on the concrete wasteland, I go hand in hand with the distant, the discourse,

It's crazy out of here; on the unloved underused lawn; sodden with remorse.

Up, down, down, down; pissing around on the concrete wasteland

As ever it was, distant and discordant.

Waiting for the time

To blow the whistle and let the fun begin:

The moment my colleagues dread.

Nuanced shrill piercing sound:

Gutting, fearsome, challenging sound

Designed to make those around stand still,

Rigid, statuesque, stuck to the ground, in theory,

But there are some who dare to breathe;

To break a move, to misbelieve

That anyone or anything can reprimand their deviance.

Soon corrected though; not on my own much longer;

Disciplinary is here, and the foot-soldiers too.

It is nice not to be alone

And I whistle again; the ranks move in line, Form by Form,
towards the battle scenes.

Left step, right step,

Year Seven First.

Wait for it Year Eleven!

Wait for it

Wait for it

Okay, go!

They've gone of course;

Come on Year Seven!

Eight, Nine, Ten,

Wait for the word.

They've heard

But gone as well.

'Nice and smooth' , someone utters,

'put down the shutters', someone flutters.

Meanwhile, I know the enemy are in their ghettos

And I groom the final sultry drag

From my naughty cigarette with the cellos singing in my ears.

Three minutes now; that's all I have,

A precious and vital amount of time to vacate the wasteland and head for the sanctuary.

It is here that I shed my coat, put on my armour, deploy my alto-ego and breathe.

But I want to go awol; I don't want to be here: far less the other side of the door

And that three minutes has become one. Then, thirty seconds, then ten:

Nine, eight, seven, six, shit, five, four, three, shit, two, one.

The division bell reverberates; I hate that sound, I feel sick.

There is not a rush to the door;

Not an unwavering demonstration of professionalism and optimism for the day ahead,

Not an overwhelming desire to educate and inspire,

Moreso an atmosphere of condemnation, cold fear and dread,

Akin to going over the top, where only sarcasm spreads

With sickening comments like 'enjoy your day', and 'into battle then' echoing in my head.

It's now two minutes since the first sounding of the bell,

There is no movement towards the impending hell.

And the General? He does not appreciate the inertia;

He storms into the sanctuary demanding that we move:

'This really is a poor example you are setting: get to your classrooms now.'

And with that, he disappears again, back to his office; never mind the children.

'Time to make a move, Chris', whispers Ellie, my empathetic assistant

Without whom I would not stand a chance.

So, I am the first to move. I reluctantly lever myself out of the chair,

Quickly adjust my hair for some quite irrelevant reason,

And edge towards the precipice,

Secure in the knowledge that once breached, I will be existing in a different world,

A different space, a frightening parallel universe where any semblance of civility

Disappears in a puff, and I know that I've had enough before I've even started.

Here I go again then; I open the door and take my first step into the corridor of uncertainty

And proceed to walk the walk of the condemned man.

My point of no return is the sixth room on the right

So the countdown begins.

The first room approaches: I hear the cacophony and now see it:

There's a fight going on, but, I do not react to it of course: not my Form;

I chastise myself concerning my obvious lack of camaraderie

But such is the state of play; I walk on by and approach the second

Whereby the same ritual is performed:

Observe the disturbance, shudder from the ferocity of the sound,

Yet do not acknowledge it: I shamefully ignore the turmoil,

And let the riot take its inevitable toll.

'Don't like that lot' says Ellie. Meanwhile, I'm feeling like jelly.

The third on the right is now approaching: the half way point of this desperate charade,

Same sounds, same sights, same anarchy, same response, same observations from Ellie:

'I don't like that lot either' she proclaims.

Then the fourth

Then the fifth.

Same everything

Same bloody everything!

But now, the game changes; the sixth door approaches.

I am but a few steps away, and I am sweating; heart-beat racing.

And it's like that with every step I take, I am not moving, I am suspended,

I am trying to delay the inevitable but I am now outside,

The classroom door is shut, but I can see inside;

There is no place to hide; with a deep breath, I prepare to meet Dracula's bride.

Eery flashback, good history books; flash, back. Not now. Flashback.

Not now, please no, not now: okay, not now;

Flash, fridge, bit: cool shit; not now. Fresh. Flesh. Find the cow

But not now; losing, sailing, diving, where's the sow?

Bubble squeak losing; my choosing, my command?

My demand and on remand.

Doc Dubbos. My Doc Doc Dubbos. My Helior!

Helior and flying fwats in a crisp packet

Embracing the scream of bats; not now Eleanor, not now Ellie!

Fort Narge, Fort Narge, Fort Narge; on repeat like Marg,

Living, speaking, Darz,

Helior: have you been wafted away to another day on Mars?

Ellie, you there? Ellie? I don't want to go in. Flash. Flash. Back.

Hundreds of bats and it's a stunning morning; full of cracks and berries and migrant birds,

So I plead; just don't touch the fun guy right now.

Listen: flash, flash, flash

Sound: back, back, back

Destroy. Destroy. Destroy,

This is nasty; it happens, just when I open the door,

This is ghastly, this is vicious, just when I'll fall through the door,

This is spacious, this is gracious; given the ultimate flaw,

This is duck-pond, this is vomit, knowing what comes before.

I know the score but it ain't a draw,

I don't want me anymore, dubbo dubbo dok dok fwats, Helior

I don't need you anymore; not now, okay, not now; what door? Evolve. Bore.

Bore-draw, nil points; the door is reluctantly, but inevitably, prised open by two lost souls,

Complete with trepidation; postponing the start of their nervous stroll.

The room seems dark, the air seems cold

But, if the truth be told, neither can be sold as accurate; what's left to behold?

'What's to behold?', you ask, ' What's to behold?'

'We are here to scold you, to burn you, to destroy you.'

Foreboding shadows lead the ritual dance; languid curtains dance with the rhythm and sway,

The withered and polished floorboards creak in sympathy as two pitiful souls wind their way.

And the silence? It is a cruel symphony; a collision of apprehension,

Unbridled angst and base intentions.

'Always the tension', you note, 'Beyond comprehension', you note,

'Yet we love the tension; we thrive on your desperation; we are your sinking boat.'

Two fragile, lifeless souls take another step and another, and another;

No one is bothered; no one greets but instead jeers of derision, doubting your mother.

The room is fraught with nightmares, with unholy scares and screams.

Two persecuted, taunted souls are part of its seams.

'As we are part of your damnation;

We are your procrastination, your assassination, your complication.'

The room remembers

Yet shows no empathy for the two vulnerable souls.

The room is always there; omnipotent, belligerent; digressed.

Anticipation? Joy? Fulfilment?

Not today; not any day.

Hey! Pupils! Leave the Teach alone; throw him a bone, or something.

Any how…..red pen ready?....black pen ready?....voice cleared by a nervous cough….?

Ritual number one of the day; repeated later.

Have I got their attention? No! Do I give a toss? No! Do I wish they'd stayed at home? Yes!

Let the battle commence. Another throat-clearing cough, and then, the words hurt me…

'Morning class; how are we today?'

The infernal din is now comprised of feral grunts and fart-like noises.

'David?' *'Grunt'* 'Ian? *'Grunt'* 'Simon?' *'Sir!'* 'Jane….Jane?' *'Not 'ere'*

The class register is not a mere enumeration, a process of surveillance and domination

That consumes the valuable time of instruction.

No. It is much more than that; it induces a collective state of sedation.

But, I ask: who's dominating, who's checking whom; who's the master of the room?

I remember being told that the class register is a mechanism of discipline

By my crusty old professor who had made good his escape many years ago.

I was informed that it was vital to monitor the attendance and punctuality

Of every child under your scrutiny, so I could punish them accordingly.

The class register, he described, was a display of authority,

Flaunting the teacher's superiority over every pupil in the learning community.

In this way, he said, you would undermine their self-esteem; putty in your hands.

The class register, he proclaimed, was more than a simple list;

It was, he surmised, a weapon of power and control.

Somehow, the reality's been missed.

Back in the moment; still reciting that endless list of names,

Still being reciprocated with grunts, inaudible comments, and those fart sounds

(You know the ones I mean: created by blowing hard on your arm; a great game.)

Finally: 'Zac?' *'Yeah baby!.'* Original I suppose. I proffer a suggestion of a smile

And conclude by saying: 'Okay; off to Assembly.' I smell riot and revolt in the gloom.

Chaos. Flying desks. Screams. Then perfect silence and an empty dishevelled room.

Lost seconds in time; lost and irretrievable black holes where everything disappears

And then, the ringing in my ears, loud and clear; the resounding force of the bell

Implores the pupils to rush to the hall, to swarm to the auditorium like crazy bees,

To sit and wait patiently for the speaker; to eagerly anticipate his oratory.

But patient they are not; nor quiet, nor placid, nor decorous.

They chatter, they giggle, they whisper; babble, snigger, murmur, shout,

They propel origami jets (an up-market version of paper planes) and deconstructed spheres,

They blatantly ignore the teachers' warnings; the mentors' admonition and pleas

Powerlessly proffered from the sides of the hall; ineffective, not moving through the gears.

They have no care at all, no fear;

Only the teachers feel fear; day after day, year after bloody year.

Here we go.

The speaker is ushered and welcomed onto the stage;

He grimaces and tries to pacify the throng

But his voice is drowned by the noise and the clamour.

He can't be heard; can't articulate his tales of glory and glamour

So, he raises his hand and shouts; begs for silence and respect

But this is like a red flag to a bull: the pupils laugh at him, mock him; jeer and deride him,

Don't listen to him at all; will not comply

And thus he loses his temper; sadly forfeits his composure,

Throws his script into the air; storms off the stage in anger

And vacates the hall in despair as his pages of wisdom settle on the floor below.

The pupils cheer and clap; confident they have won the day,

Knowing they won't pay for their riotous ways.

Then, the Head shuffles on stage, apologetically; disregards the rumpus and the fuss,

Mentions the school bus, and dismisses the gathering, as quickly as he can.

Lest I forget; whilst departing the fiasco, I recall: Period One, History, Year Nine.

This is a home fixture at my gaff; my specialist subject, my selected area of academic study,

My love. And I further recall: 'there are three of us in this marriage', she would often say,

'Teaching, History and Me.'

Loins well and truly girded, I re-enter my place,

And thirty-one reluctant scholars ignore me as if I have no trace;

'You on outer-space?' I quip, to entice even the slightest sign of scholarly attitude.

There is, of course, nothing there, there never is, just a growing sense of discontent.

An anonymous voice shouts out in an act of defiance:

'History's all about dead things, Sir.'

I perceive this utterance as a chance to interact with the motley crew:

'No, it's not. It's a rich tapestry of human beings and a celebration of their achievements.'

'History's rubbish, Sir.'

'No, it's not. It's a complex web of events and trends,

It shapes the world we live in, both our present and future ends.'

'History's boring, Sir.'

'No, it's not. It's a dynamic process of change and continuity

Which challenges our assumptions and perspectives,

It invites us to question and reflect critically.' The atmosphere takes a turn for the worse.

'History's a pile of shite; it's bollocks, it's crap………Sir.'

This is a dare, a provocation, a test of my nerve and resolve.

I pause, glance towards Ellie, consider my response, and reply.

'No, it's not. It's a relevant and personal connection,

It links us to our descendants and inspires us to act with purpose and direction.'

'Why do we have to learn History, Sir? I don't want to learn History, Sir. Can I go, Sir?'

'Why?' I respond to the agent provocateur. 'Why, why, why?' I repeat.

Sparking the class into a chorus of *'Why, why, why?'*

My tone of voice is changing; my measured reasonableness is fading; I'm sweating.

God help me; I'm floundering; my blood pressure is rising, my resolve hangs by a thread.

'If you shut up for a minute, I'll tell you why.'

Such an unprofessional answer, but it's do or die.

'History is a multiple, a contested interpretation,

History is complicated, demanding; requires collaboration;

History is expansive and inspiring…

Don't you want to expand your minds, Year Nine

Or are you just fine as you are?

Do you want to stagnate?

I throw myself into my chair; exhausted, humiliated,

I feel that I have crossed the fine line,

I've made this predicament more complicated, more threatening, than it needs to be.

I whisper under my breath:

'Look at them Ellie; they want to stagnate: they actually want to stagnate,

Do you know what, Ellie, I don't care. I do not care. I give in.'

And with the desks banging, the rulers twanging, the spittle laden blobs of paper trailing

Between pillar and post, Ellie mouths her response silently: 'Don't give up.'

But the nonsense continues and the phones come out:

'Put that phone away now or I'll confiscate it.'

'My Dad says you can't do that, Sir,' the classroom lawyer informs me,

Quickly followed by the classroom wit who shouts with feigned disgust:

'Ugh! You said "Put it away, Sir! Is it out, Sir? Is yours out, Sir?'

The laughter is soul-destroying; insulting, destructive;

I glance at the clock on the wall; forty minutes left to survive,

Then I can tell Year Nine to Sod Off, or words to that effect.

It is relentless; I trudge from one battle scene to the next,

From one bloodied field to another; from a home fixture to an away, Science, one.

Period Two has been dragged screaming away from me; it is always the case,

So, I adjust my face and prepare to enter that most unforgiving of place:

The evil residency of the cover lesson.

And the jeers start, and the howls of *'Oh No; it's him again'* attack any sense of mission.

'Cover lessons can be tricky', states the Policy, 'so perform professionally' says the Guide.

Are you kidding? I only want to hide.

'Provide an enrichening experience' states the Policy, 'be proactive' says the Guide.

You must be joking; I barely feel alive.

I feel that I've been washed up in a desolate place without the tools to survive but,

Never mind: I've got the Policy, I've got the Guide.

The Policy is full of advice. 'Get to know your pupils, walk around the class…'

I'll be walking over broken glass….

'…engage with them, be an ice-breaker, put them at ease, be assertive but approachable…'

I'll be partaking in a worthless task, a total farce.

'…then they will be able to really enjoy the lesson that lies ahead of them.'

The Guide is full of useful tips and recommendations like this.

That's the theory. Here's the practice.

My body language exudes dread; my voice is broken and weak;

I position myself behind the alien desk in the alien room, ready to preside over the alien task.

I read the alien piece of paper containing the names of the alien children needing special care,

I impart the alien instructions to the alien crowd.

'We've already done that Sir, it's in our books; look!'

I look in their books. They've already done it. They've already ticked the box.

'Do it again then, or read a book' I say. Then I proceed to look the other way.

Wonders never cease, however; miracles do happen,

The stream of consciousness which masquerades as my philosophical mind

Has been interrupted by the bell again: how I love the bell; I am one of Pavlov's dogs!

On this occasion, the bell precisely identifies the moment for the mass exodus

And ushers in one of the highlights of my professional day: 'playground' duty.

Twenty minutes of mid-morning torture, of mind-blowing irrelevance, of social insult.

'Get out there quick, Chris; have a quick puff,'

Which I do. I am now the Master of speedy ignition; I am a man possessed, on a mission

To derive as much pleasure and relief that I can muster in such a brief spell of time

Because, without reason or rhyme, I will soon be accosted by some tawdry sole

Who will take great pleasure in telling me that: *'You've been smoking, haven't you Sir?*

I can't bother lying or denying; what's the point: guilty as charged, you little mole!

Briefly, ever so briefly, I see things differently. I can digest with comparative ease

And nonchalance just what it is the Policy, the Guide, says to me about 'playground duty.'

Now positioned in the middle of the designated area, I recall these words:

'Playground Duty is a set period of time when a teacher is assigned to support pupils at play.

Playground Duty includes supervision of students in eating spaces and in the playground.'

(Logistics tell me this does not compute)

'Playground Duty is of paramount importance; it is taken seriously by the management team.'

(I bet it is, but why can they never be seen?)

'The role is to support children during their free time.'

(What about my free time: am I so insignificant as to be granted none? Oh. I see. Fine!)

'You must ensure that all areas of the playground are visible;

You must ensure that all pupils are monitored entering in and out of the building;

You must ensure that all pupils are encouraged to share and play together;

You must ensure that any incidents on the playground or dealt with fairly;

You must ensure that, at all times, you are alert and have a positive mindset.'

I do not see this as a valid scenario or a sound bet; it cannot be the case,

I feel like I am sinking without trace

As I stand in splendid isolation

Watching the colours change

And all things strange

Manifesting around me.

Strange tunes, disconnected voices,

Movement; threatening motions

Adding to the commotion.

Claims and counter-claims

Dubious games and climbing frames

And bloodied bodies, distraught refrains.

I watch. I supervise. I do not see.

I listen. I demonstrate my positive mindset

But don't believe.

'There are some boys behind the shed Sir, having a smoke.'

Somebody spoke and I went in to a dream; just like the Fab Four:

Good enough for them, good enough for me, if you get what I mean!

And I thought these words, but wanted to say them:

'Frankly, my dear, I do not give a shit: now, run along child; run along.'

It would have been obscene to utter such verbiage, plus, of course, unprofessional!

Oh My God; what am I doing here?

Windswept madness cast before me,

Revelling, cherishing the anonymity of chaos.

I am armed with a whistle, little else.

I think of the Guide again, the Policy; I can recite it well:

'Playground Duty can be a fun and rewarding experience.' Can it hell!

Little voice whispers as I and them depart the Somme:

'*Sir? Why haven't you got an award, Sir? Are you not good enough Sir? Are you crap, Sir?*'

I retort: 'what do you mean; what award?'

'*An N.T.A Sir; on "The One Show"; for good teachers Sir. You are not good, are you, Sir?*'

And do you know what? Those taunting, frivolous, cleverly barbed words, strike

Like a dagger to my heart; impact upon my psyche, hijack my train of thought, and I think

How right! The innocence of childhood revelations, spiked or not; how perverse

That I should even attempt to present an opposition, so I won't.

I am no good. I know I'm no good. I'm in my hearse already.

There is no reason for me to celebrate; I am bereft

They hit me from the right and stab me from the left

With their jibes and provocations, their chants and evocations;

What is it you want me to see?

I am tortured by these invisible wounds but I've read the script;

I am damaged goods; I drink and smoke to forget it all

In a vain attempt to walk tall and traverse the pain,

And yes, I've seen the show:

The march of the motivated, the interested, the complicated,

The parade of those with the walk, the talk; the dedicated,

The celebration of those who go above and beyond,

The suckers of whom the bosses are fond,

Those who avoid the dark side

Those who would rather bask in the light,

Those who work tirelessly to empower,

Those who give every hour. Those who say 'it's all about the kids' then 'thank you so much'

I've read the script; I've seen the show

But they both encapsulate something I do not know.

The little voice's summation appears just so.

Lessons to be learnt then: not by the kids but by me!

One, two, three: by me; painful observations, borne of the fruit of the tree

Of knowledge which ascertains, in an uncompromising fashion,

That I lack the passion, the compassion to put myself forward as a teacher:

I am more so a leech, not suited to preach,

I am not a teacher; I am not a teacher; I am not a teacher: repeat

Until the understanding's complete.

Ignore the years working on the chalk-face;

I am nothing short of a total disgrace!

I can't fill the space anymore,

I can't wait to open the door and run; far, far away,

Never to return for another day.

There are no nerves among the highly deserving winners;

A good teacher is worth a few dinners and the warm and welcoming atmosphere

Of TV land where celebrities intoxicate celebration

And the nation can see, in its collective imagination

Just what inspirations these teachers appear to be.

They are well suited and booted:

'It's not just my award,' they insist:

But they're probably pissed

Having indulged in too much fizz

From the Green Room, which they have to leave all too soon.

No nerves on show among the highly talented winners; nothing to fear:

Something to take into the next academic year.

'Give it up for your teacher', the celebrity says.

And I can hear the words that the little voice choked

'You are not good Sir, are you?' I am a failure; bespoke.

Forever selfless; that's what good teachers are,

Won't drive past you in their car;

Theirs is the gift to make you a star

So let's celebrate them; near and afar,

Yet I bear a damn awful scar,

And I question,

How did it come to this?

Seventy nine: utopia, idealism, educational dreams

Two thousand and nine: cynicism, embitterment, wondering what it means.

It has all become a massive bluff;

I have my nose in the trough

Unwillingly, but there it is

And I have had enough!

As a pupil, I loved school,

The days were short and the teachers cool

And the careers teacher, who was nobody's fool

Told me: 'One day, young Chris, so long as nothing goes amiss,

One day, you'll be a vicar or a banker; Insurance or in law,

Or a Civil Servant on the thirteenth floor

Of some swanky city hall.

However; despite your years of joy within this veritable seat of learning

Do not yield to the inevitable yearning

To be like one of us.

I have a confession. I made a mistake. Don't you make it as well.'

One afternoon, one cursed afternoon, I recall making the incorrect choice

Which, in the end, gave way to a little voice that I heard back then

But which differed from the little voice I hear right now.

Time to take my bow: time to reflect just how?

Out; I am out, I am out and about with the music dragon,

And the theatre; My God, the theatre: I want to jump back on.

I am rolling my eyes; getting up and off the stage,

It's a perfect rage and in the cage I sit and contemplate the fraud of my thoughts,

Triggering, sweetening, caressing the core people who are prepared to spill

The broken treasure in just half an hour.

Still I must check the desks and the walls for comments written on them all;

Kids laughing at my distress asking why do I sweat?

I'll bet they know; surmise the fall, and amongst them all, don't give a shit.

In the early days, I was full of optimism. Wanted to be called by my name.

Saw it as progression; saw it quite insane but there it was.

Didn't want to be a crowd controller though,

Didn't want to be a social worker, or a referee, or a cup of tea;

Didn't want to be trained in self-defence, or correctness;

Didn't want false admissions of guilt.

Didn't want to pray for the holidays

Didn't want to go into a daze but liked it.

Didn't think it was meant to be like this.

It has been a journey though; it is a unique trip with no end point,

And I am holding my poise as I walk down the stairs

Through the shouts and the scares and the ultimate dares,

Personal to me.

It is like a swimming challenge or something much colder,

Something younger, something bolder

Like a slow motion scene; a version obscene.

I am the curator; the guide, under the piano,

I assume I am a teacher but I do not know.

I'll create a page turn over!

Re-call myself; me versus me in symphony,

The sweet little ring presented in a little plastic bag

In a little plastic box with a little plastic sympathy;

Complete with my driver, I am a new volunteer,

Coughing mornings up and pulling it altogether, whatever the weather,

Consulting the engineer who says 'that is very smart.'

Starting with the fourteen dancers; the prancers of my ineptitude,

The sullen grace of being nude in spirit and wine,

I can't be fine.

The 'horror dawn' with boats and paddles and useless handles, waits for me.

It will always wait for me.

Like a tight rope across the Tower; like an ocean inspired.

Hope rise and hope fall; flat rise, flat fall,

A space to live in with eyes judging making it work.

This is entertainment city; more's the pity.

And I would rather run.

I have a very good reason,

I will hide behind a mirror

Where no one can see me,

Only my reflection; only my deception,

Only my conception of reality

Of what a marvellous teacher could be: celebrating old times

Which exhaust my nerves incessantly.

I dance with my training but it's raining:

Get inside! Get your arse inside;

Get inside and hide: run,

But you can't: I am a teacher: socially shit awkward, a troubled soul, denied.

Each and every day I think like this:

Here we go again; pick yourself up, here we go again.

It's a big deal; give me a plan and a refrain,

Give me a mindset to alleviate the plan,

But I do that myself, you know.

I mean: it was everything. It was a burnt space,

A space for my utopia where teachers weren't 'Sir' but 'Nigel' and 'Geoff'

Who, without recompense, walked into class with flippers

And snorkelling gear.

There was room for opinion; room to question what the audience said,

Chance to get inside your head and to grow up in the industry.

We pushed it all the way; we could beat the defensive issues,

No need for platitudes or a box of tissues

Because we were on the right track

And in the most dramatic of circumstances, we had their backs.

Ever since then, I've been running behind;

My positivity has been complicated;

My pro-activity sidelined;

My flag no longer flies.

So, try and retire that; try and get rid of that one with a caring soul,

Try and show him the long way out; nicely wasted,

Procrastinated, obliterated,

Well cut out; spells on loan; searching for another complication

Which ebbs and flows; develops and grows like a cancer of the soul,

Given away, intrigued, who knows

What makes a person want to teach?

What hits the credit of the players?

Why do they think that was the best decision they took?

Why didn't they read the book?

Voice; this time not little, Ellie speaks: her voice is brittle in the cold.

'You coming in Chris? You coming in?'

As I stand and peruse the scene; I'm not coming in; know what I mean?

I will be statuesque. I will let the weather and my soul and my gut take me

To a new awareness, and, in fairness, it's been coming.

I am training the noose; trying to get to the route of the problem,

Looking for the fix of contamination; I get that; cloudy in a nut shell,

Absolutely abhorring the show; trying to process the struggle.

Tidying up before I arrive, waiting for the avalanche.

And the music in my head parades memories which I'll leave for Spiderman.

There is a blanket wrapped around me with bad jokes and tales bespoke,

With a fake clap-out and an agenda.

Best be on a bender where the spotlight shines and everything's fine

In that little café, with cream teas and proper tasty coffee,

Sandwiches everywhere; fractured, manufactured, overloading the senses;

Trying to deceive; trying to believe:

Trying to signify my chosen profession,

Trying to submerge myself in the duck pond.

Without crescendo, without climax or buttons,

Without finale, or encores or futons,

Without a return to the cage,

Without my camouflage, without applause,

Without a reason and a cause

Without a bow and a tapping of the fiddle,

I am trapped in the middle of the aborted silence

With all the caveats of an aborted cure

And I'm not sure but I am buzzing like a survivor on the TV: Teacher? Be!

Exactly so: I hear the persuading voice again:

'You coming in Chris? You coming in?'

Not yet! Not just yet!

I feel like I am ballooned; unknown. On loan.

A little bit like a co-incidence, trying to relish the situation;

Trying to test the best of times; trying to live every moment,

Trying to understand the components that make me a facilitator

Or any other kind of raptor you choose to mention; procrastinator!

Did I take the right decision?

Did I fill my soul with precision?

Did I deny my own admission?

Did I put utopia over it all when I could have stood tall as a solicitor?

Or a bank clerk, or a vicar, or something much slicker?

Was I blinded by progressive ways

When we could pass the time of days with our teachers who insisted

That we used their chosen names in a sort of trendy game

Rolled up in a disguised pain; listening to the rain,

Watching the rain chase itself down the window pain.

Down, down, the rain chased itself down the windows,

Because of the windows, despite the windows,

Within the windows that I look out of now

Like a disillusioned sow,

Not knowing where to jump, and how to swim.

No conviction; no reason,

Looking for the easy life which I thought teaching would bring.

Wishing for the escape at ten past four

With the godfather and me. *'You coming in?'* Give me three.

Really? Is that all I have? What's the hurry, my dear?

I prefer to stand here and recount an industrial disease.

So, here is, the teachers' curse, in verse, if you please!

Abuse and accusation,

Burn-out, budgets, mis-conceptualisations,

Criticism, disillusionment,

Danger, warning, Mr Smith!

Excessive workloads, evaluations,

Failure. graded. Being faded,

Grim grotesque, obliterated,

Health and safety, high work-loads,

Inappropriate complaints;

Job insecurity, no justice,

Kicks and kill joy,

Lack of parental support; limited resources

(Who follows which courses?)

Morale is low; myths connect and endless meetings,

Nervousness; not a Nurse, but how are you feeling?

Ofsted? Sod Ofsted! Teachers die at the word of Ofsted,

Oppressive, obstructive, inhumane Ofsted: rather be in bed.

Paperwork: poor public people. Pointless paper tasks.

Quitting. Recruitment and Retention. Don't give it a mention; just ask.

Reports, respect, reflective practitioners;

Students bless them all; stress and standardisation,

Time limits, tantrums, tension and terror: what's your name and how's the weather?

Unreasonable demands, violence, vulnerability, sitting pretty,

Wellbeing? There is no wellbeing in the noble profession; nothing but

X-rated behaviour; yawns, yells and yob-like trailers,

Z-Car like. Zero point. Zoned: the teacher as the phaser at home.

Come in? Come in? Come into what exactly?

Come in to being a crowd controller, an entertainer, a first aider;

An advocate, a negotiator, a social worker?

An arbitrator as to whether Leslie identifies as male or female?

Come in to be what I am not,

Come in to the career that time forgot,

Come in to the eternal abuse, the mockery, the excuses?

Come in to the thirty pairs of eyes scrutinising my every move?

Come in to Rosenshine's six instructional functions,

Come in to Cantor's Assertive Discipline? Piaget?

Come in to the tragedy, the play, the act;

Come in to that scene where I continue to doubt my own credentials?

Come in to unruly students whose task it is to undermine my authority and make me sweat,

Come in to my perceived inadequacy;

Come in to disillusionment;

Come into troublesome, aggressive, uncooperative helicopter parents?

Okay, I'll come in, but really want out.

You see, in another world, another setting, another time,

I will become that toxic teacher, crawling like a snail;

Bitter, burned out, plain mean,

Retaliatory; on a mission to get my own back.

Abrasive, full of bad attitudes, prone to fits of uncontrollable shouting and raging

With the ultimate desire to humiliate and degrade,

A yearning to do nothing that will improve myself,

And a motivation to be a silent bully,

In cahoots with my role as the toxic teacher,

Not abused, but feared; not mocked but feared; not judged: simply feared;

The epitome of the reflective practitioner:

Shaken but not stirred; mirrored but not inferred. I will be truly in, then.

'Ursula, bless her; did you see her today?

Prancing about like a miniature street-walker, with her skimpy clothes and nose ring?'

'What about Lance? Dyed and spiked hair; shuffling about in baggy jeans,

Resplendent in the process of just falling off!'

'And the playground resembled killing fields at break!'

'Systematically rampant, I think the expression is!'

'Twelve year olds; they're sodding twelve years old!'

So goes a typical conversation in a typical staff-room in a typical teachers' lunch break

And I don't want to hear it!

Just what is it that persuades teachers, in their down time, to discuss issues of work?

I, for one, just want to switch off, albeit temporarily;

I want to escape the ravages of Ursula and Lance,

I want to disappear; I need to disassociate myself from this daily diatribe;

I plead for a cool phase.

This lunchtime, as every lunchtime, cliques assemble in their assumed spaces,

Souls contort and people's faces pass the time of day in a peculiar way

Which obliterates any sense of recovery.

Idle words and careless anecdotes pervade and continue like a fruitless whisper;

Doesn't matter what people say. Everyone agrees anyway.

Not me though, not me; I become unsociable me;

I hide behind yesterday's paper and yesterday's news.

I express no views about Year Nine or Ten,

Or the relative benefits of Buddhist Zen.

I embrace the odour of yesterday's left-over curry,

I take solace in curled up sandwiches and uninspiring salads in plastic boxes.

I escape for a smoke and dream again,

Waiting for the bell to sign that lunch break is over, again.

Right now though, the dream is over, temporarily; like confetti

It blows and lingers in the wind then disappears, and opens up new fears

About the next few hours. But: there comes in all of us teachers,

A time to not be preachers, or seekers, or pleasers, but a chance to be chameleons,

Masters of disguise, as we hide behind the mask; an opportunity to laugh

And that chance comes in a brief passing window, known as afternoon registration.

Half way through the day, right? Soon be tonight, right? Soon be over, right? Right!

Celebration in the air; cool-shit Simon combs his hair, but do I care: sod it; No,

I positively glow, as I begin my deep-dive into silliness: you know!

'Late again Simon then? What's it this time? A flood of biblical proportions?

Alien abduction; earthquake, volcano, hurricane, tsunami; lost your mummy?'

The class don't get it. It falls flat like a pancake; my humour is aborted and lost.

I used to be able to make a class laugh at such a comment;

I had rapport; they knew I liked to joke around and tease.

Once, they were pleased with me; now, they don't understand,

They rain on my plan; not at ease.

And the clipboards were there, the suited, booted, clipboards

Who waft around the place in disguised disgrace;

Their role: to escape the chalk-face but bring their colleagues down;

Passing opinion with a deathly frown and a private snigger nonetheless.

'You are too sarcastic; you do not show respect; take a little while to reflect.

You upset your pupils; you deny their innocence. You are flippant; offensive,

You put them on the defensive; you poke fun, you are upsetting them;

You erode their trust. Please modify your behaviour.'

My God! My Saviour! What has this job become?

State the time; two forty, known as Period Five; the last shot at the day: Okay?

The bell, the siren, the chimes, iterate in my head; almost there, almost bed.

Fifty minutes to come, fifty minutes to go like a lava flow,

Like a best case scenario; like a jingle comes and flows;

Blurred, conscripted, unvalued, journeyed.

Fucking Period Five: don't want to be there as the windows sweat,

They don't, I don't: ring, ring, place a bet;

Don't want to play the game, or hit the horse of course,

Don't give a toss about GCSE this afternoon: want to go home.

The pupils before me are bereft; they don't want to know,

Wishing the rain would change to snow.

Home bell they beg and say and plead

And I, as the teacher, bleed in solidarity.

Period Five; lost in the divide, listening to those who cried:

'Long live the divide'

Sing sing sing, bling bling bling, thing thing thing,

Hide!

Fabricate, procrastinate, disguise my eyes,

I cannot wait for the end of Period Five.

I'm supposed to be the teacher; I'm supposed to educate,

I'm assumed to care

It's not fair; the responsibility placed on me,

But, hey, fifty minutes gone,

Let's sing another song and wave the kids goodbye.

Let's have another try tomorrow,

Let me fly.

Each and every day, about this time of day, I put in this request:

Let me fly! Let me go!, and for a split second, my soul is raised

But not today; I have just remembered: today is the occasion of the double-whammy!

I am in detention! And there's a staff meeting! Unrestricted joy!

I am not a fan of detention duty or detaining anyone, but I am in a rota to do it:

To supervise the most sought-after post-school club of all,

Membership of which is a badge of honour,

Attendances at which are sought like trophies! The perceived miscreants stand tall

In the confines of the detention hall, witnessed by the lined-up revelling the fall.

I present as a teacher, an educator: I am not in favour of imprisonment or incarceration,

Confinement or captivity, internment or custody,

Restraint or apprehension, constraint or subjugation.

I am not a gaoler, terrorist, or Police Officer,

But I might as well be, as I sit in front of a group of outlaws – desperadoes –

Intent of having a jolly good time at my expense

Who take great pleasure in ignoring my plea for silence

As they go about their numbingly boring and futile punishment tasks

Such as 'write an essay about the reasons for my detention,'

Or 'write five hundred lines – I must behave in class.'

Their eyes are locked on me; my discomfort is sensed, the cue for mayhem apparent.

And the paper flies, the swear words fill the room, the laughter and the jeering

Send shudders down my spine. Thirty minutes of torture ensues.

And I ask: just who is it that is in this detention; this arbiter of restorative justice?

These children have no intention of reflecting on their misdemeanours:

They are there for a laugh and a giggle and a poke at my sanity.

This is not what I signed up for all those years ago; I'm being taken to the cleaners.

Where did my utopia go? Why is it so? Do I want to know? Not really; not at all.

Time gone, show over; let them go into the shower

For now it is the hour of detention number two; one of quite a few,

Commonly referred to as the staff meeting,

A chance for professional catch-up, to spread the educational news.

And I can grab a quick smoke, before the ritual blues.

It was never like this: we were given a sporting chance;

A time to prepare for the challenging dance.

Yes: the phone call had been received; the information retrieved,

That the Ofsted inspectors were in town and that in six weeks

We were in the firing line.

But, we had warning, and, after the dawning, we got in earlier and left late,

Books were marked in green ink; lesson plans and meetings were great,

Policies were updated, value created; everything was created

So we'd succumb the test and quash our anxiety.

Not now: rather this. We are informed of just a day's notice

Then they will judge us after just two days; my mind is phased,

Is numbed, just like the turkeys detained with me;

Praying to be free; pleading to be free.

This is not a cool ride anymore; not a neat trip,

Nothing to do with the published script,

Nothing to do with the ensemble,

Nothing to do with rationality.

We are fodder to be judged; we need cold water therapy;

Think I'll pull a sicky tomorrow|: well-practiced like a stoat

But that is not fair so perhaps I won't:

I need to get onboard a boat

And float away, insignificantly, surfing the strangled moat.

Hiatus, pause, break: intake of breath; a few mumbled comments, then:

Flight, retreat, withdrawal, evacuation,

Exit, leaving, mass migration,

Departure, diaspora, emigration, gush,

Hegira, outflow, outpour, rush,

Outflowing, outpouring, retirement, run,

Egression, escaping; the starting gun,

Fleeing, journeying, outward going, stream,

De-camping, re-locating, living the dream,

Getaway, procession, chicken run fun!

Procession, movement, scramble,

Barnstorm, issue, ramble,

Pissed off,

Exodus.

Exodus of the people.

Exodus of the professionals,

Exodus of the noble professionals;

Moaning, groaning, citing waste of time,

And it's a crime: so undignified, and the words don't rhyme.

Exodus: a sudden departure of a large number of professionals

From a meeting they were obliged to end.

Exodus: a state of streaming out rapidly, sometimes figuratively,

Into the darkness, in to which they blend

Anonymously, distressed, driven round the bend.

But, not me; not me yet; I need to re-generate,

I need to become human again;

I need to have a drink and have a smoke,

I need to sense the rain.

'Okay? You okay Ellie? : can't leave right now; just not ready.

Ellie; want to join me? Want to feel the cold? Want to guess the pain?

Yes? That's good. It's a comfort; can't go right now;

I have to wait; feel the rain: look out for the next reframe,

Got to ride the majesty blame.

Want a smoke? No? Grab a coffee? No?:

Listen to me? Okay. In the rain? Okay?

I'm not holding you up, am I?

No? You sure? No? Don't mind if I? No? Won't tell? No? Not sure?'

Pure imagination; total trust and condemnation; tears ripping down my face

With sheer exaggeration and something like disgrace.

Emotionally sobbing, vessels throbbing,

Fifteen hundred people on the curb, describing the mad absurd

Asking, begging: let me have a look,

Let me be the master cook.

'Sorry boring you, Ellie? Anything to watch on telly?

Can't leave right now. If you're sure, Ellie, but I must go soon:

What a shitty afternoon!' ' I know.' 'How do you know?' 'I was there.'

'Of course you were; the angel in the room.

Sure you don't want to join me? Will take you pains away;

No? You sure? It's just another day!

No? Fine. I respect your choice,

Your magnificence and your voice,

But, excuse me right now, as I chill out nice and slow

Watching the coffee beans grow

And waiting for the rain to end

Which of course, it won't: I know.'

Sad. I am so sad; It's sort of yeah and feeling bad,

Digging sense and going mad;

Something like I've never had;

Expression in my hands.

Oh yes, of course, I put on a hell of a show

Once, back then, when all the garden grew,

Like there was something

I never guessed or knew.

First day: I was mistaken for a kid;

Get off your bike, the teacher said,

Walk it to the yard!

Yes sir, I said, and did as I was told.

Really sorry to hold you up my friend;

I've come to the bitter end;

Hope I did not offend your sensibilities.'

'Of course not, but I must go':

'Me too, me too, must be so:

Caretaker's waiting to shut up shop,

Just get my books; I mustn't stop,

A fun night awaits me: Civil War and World War One,

Loads of red ink; have some fun!

You?' 'Just me and the kids. Bolognese and picked squids!'

'Really?' 'No, made that up! I'll have vodka in the cup!'

'Enjoy then.' 'I will.' 'See you.' 'Goodnight.' 'Bye.' 'Bye.'

She's gone; they've gone, feeling high,

Something else I have to try,

But right now, I shuffle into my car,

Ready to drive; hit the show, cook the roasted potato.

Exit left, exit right, exit right and centre;

That's what the play production notes dictate;

That's how they feel and seen you mate;

How they sage and miscreate, ready for the sound.

And there it goes: the clock-timed bell,

The ringing hell; incessant, pleading, leaving, bell,

But the only difference is: most have gone, most have gone to hell,

Most have stories more to tell;

Most, just most, have gone; most will sing the song.

Exit left, exit right and centre;

I want to but I'm just an offender.

I need to hear the bell ring out,

I have to feel its heavy clout.

I guess that what it's all about; it

Is the incessant ringing: ring ring ring ring ring ring ring; out of hours,

Incessant ringing but school is out,

And I don't give a fig if the caretaker has to stop it;

I don't care a little tiny bit.

I need to exit right and centre, and left:

I am desolate: I must escape the bell which has no cause at all.

Ring, ring: fucking ring: I hear you but ignore you,

You cannot make me a prisoner; can't hold me against my will.

I am in my car; ready to escape the grip of contemplate,

I will drive. I will be free, only to be a prisoner again.

Isn't that great!

Not really; no. Life goes to and fro,

Life has nothing to know,

About the ultimate demise of a teacher and the potato.

You know the guy: the preacher, man. Drive baby, drive.

While I recall what's written on the back of an Iceland receipt;

It's all so cool with no deceit, it is a deep dive complete

With head material, offering the escape,

Searching for the other landscape.

I am now driving baby; driving, hiding, recognising

That certain positions have put me in this situation,

And I don't want an actor to recreate my actions,

You wouldn't want a thespian to fly a plane;

You wouldn't want to go insane without some recompense

Like sitting on a fence, with splinters up your arse.

Drive baby to the bridge: the point of entry, the point of 'go.'

The village and the streets that flow

Towards the river; deep piercing shiver

Pulses through my veins; a ghost delivers

My glance at the reason, the untold most treason

Of being a teacher.

And as I drive, I'm struggling with the moment;

Can't figure out what's right or ill-defined:

I'm playing sparkles in my mind,

Researching teachers lives, academically in line.

Then, I reach the bridge: it took me in, now shits me out;

As I cross, I check the tourists' shout

Of never be a teacher, see. Never be a teacher: flee,

Run, run, run away: choose yourself another day,

Inhale the different coloured smoke of another way.

You are a teacher: you are over the bridge. There's no turn-about.

How could there ever be? I'm off the bridge and roaming free,

And my mind is travelling with the car, inside the car, outside the car,

Running, fleeing, flying; soaring high above the trees and the mis-believes;

Seeking the juxtapose and the creeds that spoke to me before

I pledged my soul and went too far, I suppose, like a tree grows then sheds its leaves.

Back in seventy-nine, I met myself on the job;

I was a wonderful person, a fun guy like a mushroom, a real Socialist!

I jumped on and off the roundabout; believed the images,

I believed I was going to be a great teacher but I was pissed!

Never mind that: I was full of values; embraced the moral nature of teaching,

Filled with good spirit, team spirit and radical leanings;

Consumed with atmosphere and understanding,

Supported the cause of genuine interaction.

I listened, I acted. I was present. I co-operated,

Mine was the mission, the moral endeavour:

I embraced all: the challenged and the clever in some utopic nation,

I personified the passion, the fashion, for progressive education.

I was the original reflective practitioner; full of contemplation.

I encapsulated the community of the classroom back in seventy-nine

And everything was fine; like a glass or two of cheap red wine.

Mine was the passion; I thought I was in fashion and down with the kids,

Despite their taunting and obvious fibs.

I was whole-hearted and kind; vaguely un-defined;

Virtuous, empowering, open and kind;

Expressive, intuitive, the lighter of the spark,

Visionary, a dreamer with extraordinary imagination.

Back in seventy-nine, I had it all,

A real kind of tenderness and empathy, before the fall.

Onwards then; forward I go, away from my imprisonment, toward the roads that flow

To my temporary sanctuary; the bosom I call home where all is right

And peace, and bliss, and loveliness grow in equal measure:

Something is right; something is treasured; somewhere to sooth my battered ego.

It is not seventy-nine anymore; that year lies shattered on the floor;

Guess I face the exit door.

I am two-layered, two people; too ill-disposed, too sore;

I am the artificial teacher: I can give no more.

Low on enthusiasm, devoid of motivation; frustrated, berated,

Overwhelmed, understated, nothing simple, always complicated.

I am burnt out by demands, commands, and expectations,

Feel unsupported, isolated; unappreciated.

I lack autonomy: it's not like it used to be,

When teaching was fun and full of creativity.

It's now about workload, high stakes, accountability,

Lack of recognition, denial, pupil accusations.

The joy has gone: it's a battle scene, where there used to be beauty and love.

And they say: all you need is to seek advice; take the pill and pay the price,

Be mentored, re-charge; it will be nice!

Re-connect with the purpose, the values, the ethics of teaching,

Take up a hobby: discover the meaning!

And I ask: to whom are you preaching, creep;

Stuff the analysis: weep!

How I long for seventy-nine; naïve perhaps, but all was fine,

It was such a golden, optimistic, idealistic, no holds barred, time;

There was no crime at all.

Destiny perhaps, but no reason – no rhyme,

Nothing like the red-white line,

Nothing confined and realised; nothing like a point in time,

Simply because I have re-invented the person; got another version of me,

Climbed the everlasting tree.

I see it all now as I drive; I am alive, but dead;

Wondering just what I said.

Living a life of inertia; Stillness in my Armageddon.

Red lights, green lights, exit, go:

The beauty of it all says, it's not so!

Green lights, red lights, hold on, stop:

Reflect, passive: don't you know?

Teacher boy; teacher boy; give yourself a chance,

Teacher boy, teacher boy, you deserve another dance.

Techer boy: you searched for the meaning,

You sought out the truth and the utmost deep feeling,

And you were appealing in those early days

Of rhythmic postulations and craziest ways.

There was an element of fate in your perusal,

There was an open gate in your refusal.

Teacher boy; teacher toy – have another glance

At the road; somehow, you are approaching home.

Open the script, read the tome.

Carefully, mindfully, I turn into my drive:

I am home now; I can come alive.

Stop the car, ignition off; belt off, get out, lock:

How you feeling? Okay, cock?

Enter.

Time to enter.

Something doesn't feel right;

Return to sender.

I fumble for the keys and wave at people passing by;

Something's out of sight,

Feel like I've been on a bender.

Got the right key; turn the lock,

How you feeling? Not right, cock!

Open the door; kick aside the post

And there is a sense of wrongness.

No light. No breath. No circumstance;

No 'how's your Mum?', no recompense.

Nothing but a stale smell,

Nothing but a guide to hell;

Nothing but the ringing of a delusional bell.

I fumble for the switch,

I illuminate proceedings,

I shout my normal Norwich greetings

But there is no response, and then, OMG,

I see it all, the Salsa damage; the crippling dark realisation:

Lucy in the sky with demons and all that.

I witness devastation.

Fifteen coffee mugs, half discarded with dregs,

Filth and dust and gaping holes where the fridge once was,

And the cooker, and the table, and the photo of Lady Mabel;

The house is gutted; my textbooks strewn across the floor

Complete with the exercise books I should have marked before I left.

Total and utter carnage; my home is wrecked.

I survey the rancid scene – is this just a terrifying dream? No. It's real. I have checked.

Never at home have I witnessed such a stage of riotous incarnation,

Of condemnation or exasperation. No. I am deflected; I am the person checked

For distortions, absolutions; put me in the cradle so I can rock me gently asleep.

I call out her name: no reference to Anglian town. No refrain: no gown, no procrastination;

All I can do is weep, and light up, and imagine, and imagine and smoke and smoke.

Go far, engineer; check out the mediation session; I'm full of understanding;

I'm sure, yeah, I trust the intention,

And what's your first thought? Is it right? Does it flow meandering?

Does it have a new conception?

Am I facing a burglary? The initial scene would suggest so;

Smoke baby smoke; pour a drink, dream; find the in-between, truth must grow,

But there are coffee cups, loads of discarded coffee cups:

Burglars would not leave coffee cups; they don't have time for a coffee,

Let alone in cups.

Draw, puff; draw, puff; draw, run up the stairs;

Run down the stairs. Seen the same devastation there,

Run up and down, up and down, echoing primeval scream:

You there? You in my dream? Can you be seen? Where are you?

Flashback: something was not right this morning;

You were anxious, obtuse, like something dawning,

Then it hits me, without warning; without chance and without scorning:

She has left me. She has ripped up my BA, my MA, my PGCE,

My threshold certificate, my destiny, and left them incarcerated on the floor: my 'me'.

And now I sense an intoxicating colour

And now I see, enact and breathe, the free-fall colour:

Yellow. This is the colour I conceive; this is the colour I must mute.

It offers false signposts, but illuminates the route,

Tells me when to wear my finest two-tone suit.

Cadmium yellow; rhymes with bellow and fellow,

Also rhymes with secret bordello.

It is the colour of my front door, the colour of my car,

The colour of destruction, the colour of the bar.

There is a ribbon of this designation wrapped round a mature tree.

There is a dessert topping oozing from how a canine sees,

There are brick roads and large taxis; cartoon submarines,

All can be, all can be. Anything you want it to be.

Bellies, rivers, daffodils,

Cowardice; to the woods and over the hills;

Different coated sugared pills

Designed to beat all ills; in theory, anyway, depending on the day.

Known for its calming personality, like the tones of a cello:

I'm referring to the colour yellow.

And what else is yellow? What wears the coat?

The all sublime, sad, post-it note.

On the table, among the coffee mugs and biscuit crumbs,

I spy two such incarnations and I go numb.

One reads: let's remember the good times and forget the bad.

The other concedes: there were three of us in our marriage;

You, me and your mistress, aka calling: that's what wrecked our carriage.

I am broken, shattered; my life's been splattered by something that's essentially wrong;

She's singing the wrong lyrics, got the wrong song: but, there it is, in yellow, she's gone.

It only sounds appropriate of course. Did that really happen?

Was it a surreal dream? Did you make it simple, if you know what I mean,

Did you make it swing?

I am a bloke for detail; I get the scream,

I feel the emptiness as I survey the scene.

I chat to the lady in the lift who says: turn the TV off,

And I speak to the one I know as Mrs McGough.

I search for week five, and week six, with additional resources,

I reason with horses, and chances, and courses,

And I pray: don't let my accent change; my brain explode or re-arrange,

Let it fade, person, let it degrade. As if for you I had been made.

Without you, it's a different story: sit you down while I sketch;

I'm slightly nervous what you'll have to fetch. It's a stretch

Of credibility, insanity: get your dog to fetch the remnant I forbade.

Such charisma; such talent. You hold life in the balance;

Fancy a drink? Speak to the talents!

Smash a window as our son once said. Why have you left
our carnal bed?

Was it something I thought about you or said? Or me and
my teaching?

Did I pontificate? Was I preaching? Go from zero to five?

Was I dead, or barely alive?

You have snapped the ruler; couldn't be much crueller;

You have attacked the picture and the tutor;

You have got it so wrong,

And I don't know where I belong

Any more. I cannot survive, any more.

Transfixed; that just about summarises my state of mind before the final bow,

Forty years of nothingness comes to something now;

Schon will be proud of me as I reflect upon the dereliction of regret:

As I hit the bum notes and self-deflect.

This is the termination point of the rhyme, circumspect and what's my crime?

And there's no reason, neither time, to declare I'm alright. I have no fight. No sign.

You cite a mistress – never had one; you cite a three-some, never was one –

You are so away from the truth. I never had fun.

You talked of good times and talked of bad; wrong lyrics, wrong titles, wrong opposite sum!

So; what to do?: nothing. What to say? : nothing. What to be?: nothing. To pray?: nothing.

So; why? Nothing. So, when? Nothing. So, who? Nothing. So how?: nothing.

I just don't know; I don't know, I bloody don't know, I don't know: there is nothing.

On the floor, amongst the debris, is a discarded folder: an old Ofsted report. To make it bolder

I underlined key phrases in yellow: clear vision, pride, calm, orderly, purpose: now, I'm older.

These were not love letters to myself, nor reminders of a steamy affair,

They were persuaders, infiltrators, prompts to make me not too scared,

Nothing to suggest that I did not care for you: I loved you, not my calling that never was.

You got it sadly wrong: wrong lyrics, wrong song.

Ellie? You there? Ellie? I need to talk right now,

Ellie? Dear Ellie? Will you wipe my fevered brow?

Ellie? Sweet Ellie? You can't; you're not in my bed,

Ellie? Fictitious Ellie? You reside in my head!

So, I will have another drink and another smoke;

It will be like somebody spoke to me and said:

This is it: your life and your story laid bare, you sorrowful teacher. Wait for the bell again.

X-rated post production notes, total obliteration, battlefield avenue:

The preceding diatribe has been a Chris Moore creation

Whereby reality has been bent tested and shaken,

Just like the state of the great British nation.

What has gone before has been a 'shamed disgrace' production,

In association with 'hands over the face,'

'Looking through the microwave,'

'Shouldn't have said that' and 'What's the point?' incorporated.

Screenplay was in association with 'post-it notes': colours unleashed which

Can utter a lie or two, and ask: who are you?

Direction by: lived it, sensed it, guessed it, knew,

Walking in-between the few, pissing in the sink of the old vampire school.

It was make believe, of course; was it? Pupils ready? – oh yes; Teachers ready? – oh no,

Like a special occasion; which bit? Can't say so, don't know! But, I can flow

With a special appearance by the most welcomed guests of all: the extras.

Of all though, I must thank the director, the respecter

Who read it, and got it, and understood; the receptor

Valued for the input and the marvellous spectre

Entertaining me until the fall: you contradictory deflector.

Yes; I might have worn the hood; got myself in with the brotherhood,

With an obstinate sense of reason, but I never guessed I could

 Have traversed the route, if only for the greater good.

I am the A.I Teacher; peruser of the ill-conceived;

X-rated position with nothing retrieved and no-one to believe. I took the hit,

Like I should, it was the perfectly uncompromising final bit.

Xanadu? It never was; it never could have been.

Nirvana? No, but the teen spirit was there; mine and theirs.

Fights on the stairs, broken chairs,

Spittle, swearing, riotous scenes.

Xanadu?, not a chance!

I've partaken of the most sinister of dances

Over my pedagogic years.

And now, amongst the pushing and the shoving,

Where I once hoped for kindness and loving,

Is nothing but cruelty, postponement and fear;

Nothing but dangerous tendencies,

Ransacked rooms and ripped off wall displays,

Assaults and punch-ups and other various affrays;

It was never meant to be this way

But it is.

I'm glad I don't see 'dystopia rules' scrawled upon the blackboard any more.

I'm grateful that I'm not one of the five who have been hit,

I'm oblivious to the score,

I'm out of the shit.

And I'm not going to break back into the room with a cricket bat,

I'm not going to sit there and be abused like that;

My days surviving the everlasting battle, I'll leave to the odious cattle

Who masquerade as parents and give it all the chat, whilst I am sat

Vulnerable behind a desk in the hall, irrelevant to it all.

They've had a drink and had a smoke; in copious quantities,

I'm assaulted by the fumes of questionable quality.

So, *I* will have a drink and a smoke too, it's the end of the chase,

And prepare myself to sink without trace,

Wondering what happened to that idyllic, exotic, luxurious place.